## The Sunny Day Squad

# THE QUEST FOR THE CARINGSTONE

Written by **Michael Panzner**
Illustrated by **Polly Mooney**

Twin Unicorn Publishing LLC, Tampa, Florida

Dedicated to all those
who bring joy to our lives.

Published by Twin Unicorn Publishing LLC
Tampa, Florida
www.twinunicornpublishing.com

Library of Congress Control Number: 2023951516

ISBN: 979-8-218-29081-8
(paperback)

This book belongs to:

_____

Under the golden sun of Gaggle Grove,
where daffodils dance and honeybees hum,
live four close friends.

Known as The Sunny Day Squad, they use their special talents to bring joy to the world.

Ollie the monkey can navigate the trickiest terrains.

Poppy the puppy loves charming people with silly rhymes.

Daisy the rabbit makes magical songs out of thin air.

And Ted the horse likes turning ordinary items into really useful stuff.

One day, Ollie, Poppy, Daisy and Ted were playing hide-and-seek near the old oak tree when Gaggle Grove began buzzing with excitement. Whispers spread about the Squad's next adventure. Children gathered, eyes wide open, wondering what awaited their heroes.

Suddenly, a winded explorer named Captain Bravebutter appeared, clutching a wrinkled scroll. A parrot named Pete clung to his shoulder, his little head tilted forward. The Captain's eyes gleamed with a mix of weariness and anticipation as he slowly unrolled an ancient map.

"Behold, dear Sunny Day Squad!" the visitor exclaimed. "This document reveals the location of the fabled Caringstone, a remarkable gem that can make even the saddest child smile."

A magical figure had appeared in his dream, the Captain said, urging him to go find the Caringstone so he could help all the little ones in need.

"But I cannot embark on this dangerous quest alone,"
he explained. "I need your help!" With their hearts racing
and eyes twinkling, Ollie, Poppy, Daisy and Ted eagerly agreed.

Soon, they were heading through the forest. Ollie swung from branch to branch, leading them on with a big bright smile. The others followed, with Poppy at the rear, her tail wagging like a conductor's baton.

Piddly pump, let's all jump,"

he shouted. "Mind the stumps and watch the bumps!" Her

lue eyes sparkled with optimism, keeping everyone's spirits high.

After a while, they came upon a large and lazy llama who blocked their way. They looked at each other, wondering what to do.

Ollie made a silly face and said, "please excuse us," but the llama just sat there and snoozed. They worried they might have to turn back because he simply wouldn't move.

In less than no time, Daisy leapt into action.

She grabbed a stick and tapped out a bouncy beat.

She swung a shell through th air, echoing a twinkly tune.

She sang a song about prancing and dancing, and suddenly the llama was on his feet.

Caught up in the excitement, he took off like a crazy loon.

"Music guides us," Daisy mused, her ears swaying softly to the rhythm in her head.

It wasn't long before the group faced another challenge. Stopped in their tracks by a deep and choppy river, they weren't quite sure what to do. Soon, Poppy had a plan. She called out to some beavers nearby who were building a dam.

"Hello, you talented timber technicians, are you having a nice day?" she asked. "Would you mind helping us get across so we can continue on our way?"

The beavers hesitated at first, until Ollie jumped in. He bounced around and flipped upside down, giving them quite a show.

This made them laugh and they agreed to help. In only minutes, they made a walkway over the water with branches, leaves and mud.

"See, we are bridge builders!" Poppy giggled.
"With teamwork, niceness, and great big smiles,
we can cover lots of miles."

The group waved goodbye and continued on their journey. They soon found themselves at the base of a cliff, with no clear way up.

This time, it was Ted who came up with a plan. Why not put together a climbing rope, he thought, with some sticks, stones and vines that were lying around?

"Where there's a will, there's a way," Ted said, as he quickly got to work.

When everything was firmly in place, he began pulling himself up, followed by the others.

At the top, they found what they were looking for. Bathed in the sun's bright light, the Caringstone sparkled like a star.

Their cheers filled the air as Ollie carefully placed the gem into the Captain's hands. Pete the parrot squawked loudly as they all turned around and headed home.

Back in Gaggle Grove, a grand feast awaited them. The community gathered round, filled with warmth and admiration.

Captain Bravebutter stepped forward, expressing his heartfelt thanks to the four great friends. "You found the Caringstone because of your bravery, cleverness, teamwork and determination," he cheered. "You are truly heroes!"

That night, as they got ready to go to sleep in their treehouse, Ollie, Poppy, Daisy and Ted reflected on the day's adventure.

Poppy yawned, rubbing her eyes. "We succeeded because we were there for each other," she said.

"And we made the most of our talents," Ted added.

"But most importantly," Daisy exclaimed, "we never gave up."

"Of course!" said Ollie, with his silly grin. "We're the Sunny

Printed in Great Britain
by Amazon

36376025R00021